# HELPING YOUR BRAND-NEW READER

## Here's how to make first-time reading easy and fun:

▶ Read the introduction at the beginning of the book aloud. Look through the pictures together so that your child can see what happens in the story before reading the words.

▶ Read the first page to your child, placing your finger under each word.

▶ Let your child touch the words and read the rest of the story. Give him or her time to figure out each new word.

▶ If your child gets stuck on a word, you might say, *"Try something. Look at the picture. What would make sense?"*

▶ If your child is still stuck, supply the right word. This will allow him or her to continue to read and enjoy the story. You might say, *"Could this word be 'ball'?"*

▶ Always praise your child. Praise what he or she reads correctly, and praise good tries too.

▶ Give your child lots of chances to read the story again and again. The more your child reads, the more confident he or she will become.

▶ Have fun!

Text copyright © 2000 by Leda Schubert
Illustrations copyright © 2000 by William Benedict

First edition 2000

Library of Congress Cataloging-in-Publication Data
Schubert, Leda. Winnie all day long / Leda Schubert ;
illustrated by William Benedict.—1st ed.
p.    cm.
Summary: Winnie the dog awakens everyone in the
house, goes in and out, takes a walk, and finally
falls asleep everywhere except in her bed.
ISBN 0-7636-1041-0
[1. Dogs—Fiction.] I. Benedict, William, ill. II. Title.
PZ7.S38345    Wh 2000
[E]—dc21        99-048485

2 4 6 8 10 9 7 5 3 1

Printed in Hong Kong

This book was typeset in Letraset Arta.
The illustrations were done in gouache.

Candlewick Press
2067 Massachusetts Avenue
Cambridge, Massachusetts 02140

# WINNIE ALL DAY LONG

CANDLEWICK PRESS
CAMBRIDGE, MASSACHUSETTS

**Leda Schubert**  ILLUSTRATED BY **William Benedict**

# Contents

# WINNIE WAKES UP

1

# Introduction

This story is called *Winnie Wakes Up*. It's about how Winnie the dog wakes up Annie and how Annie wakes up Mommy and Daddy.

Winnie wakes up.

4

Winnie sits by Annie's bed.

Winnie barks.

Winnie jumps on Annie's bed.

7

Annie wakes up.

8

Annie wakes up Mommy and Daddy.

9

Now everybody is up.

Winnie is happy.

# IN AND OUT

# Introduction

This story is called *In and Out*.
It's about how Winnie the dog makes
Mommy, Daddy, and Annie let her
in and out, over and over again.

Winnie wants to come in.

Daddy lets her in.

15

Winnie wants to go out.

16

# Mommy lets her out.

17

# Winnie wants to come in.

18

# Annie lets her in.

Winnie wants to go out.

"NO!" say Mommy, Daddy, and Annie.

# WINNIE'S WALK

## Introduction

This story is called *Winnie's Walk*.
It's about all the things Winnie the dog
does to get Mommy and Daddy and
Annie to take her for a walk.

Winnie wants a walk.

24

**Winnie wags her tail.**

25

# Winnie gets her leash.

26

**Winnie holds her leash.**

# Winnie barks.

Winnie barks MORE.

Winnie barks **A LOT MORE.**

Winnie gets a walk.

# WINNIE'S BEDTIME

# Introduction

This story is called *Winnie's Bedtime*. It's about all the places Winnie the dog sleeps until she finds the best bed.

33

# Winnie is sleepy.

Winnie sleeps on the rug.

Winnie sleeps under the table.

**Winnie sleeps on Mommy's chair.**

Winnie sleeps on Daddy's lap.

38

Winnie sleeps on the stairs.

Winnie sleeps on Annie's bed.

40

# Annie sleeps in Winnie's bed.